To.
My JuJu
I Love you To The
max.

YOU WILL DO GREAT THINGS

BY
AMERIE

ILLUSTRATED BY
RAISSA
FIGUEROA

ROARING BROOK PRESS
NEW YORK

You will do great things
Wherever you may go.

You will do daring things—

HELLO GRANDMOM AND GRANDDAD! 사랑해요!

BEAR

SUNDA[Y] FUNDAY!

FAMILY REUNION FAREWELLS

BALANCE BIKE PRO!

It's something that I know.

You will do cool things—

The way you step, smile, and move . . .

Because you'll dance
to your own song,

Your own special groove.

You will do strange things

But hold tight to your vision
So maybe, one day, they can.

You will try new things
That might feel too hard to grasp,

But don't give up—just try again,
And you'll succeed at last.

You will travel far and wide.

You may get lost out there.

You might not know
what's up or down,
But be still. Be aware.

Listen for that teeny voice

That's always been inside.

It will help you find your way.

Trust it to be your guide.

'Cause life is what you make it.
There's so much you can do.

I promise you'll surprise yourself
If you believe in you.

You will do big things
That just might change the world.

And you will do small things
That may help one boy or girl.

You will be the things
Those before us couldn't be.

And you will carry in your heart
The power of their dreams.

Be bold,
   be strong,
       my dreamer,
           Whatever you may choose.

I know you'll do great things,
Because greatness is in you.

And I will be here always
To help you spread your wings,

To watch you rise, to watch you soar,
To watch you do
Great things.

For my mother, Mi Suk, and my father, Charles.
For Granddad Charles, Grandmom Jin Yub, and the ancestors.
And for River, my blessed son, my shining star.
—A. M. M. N.

Dedicated to those who don't let me fall short.
—R. F.

Published by Roaring Brook Press
Roaring Brook Press is a division of Holtzbrinck Publishing Holdings Limited Partnership
120 Broadway, New York, NY 10271 • mackids.com

Library of Congress Control Number: 2022906886

Our books may be purchased in bulk for promotional, educational, or business use.
Please contact your local bookseller or the Macmillan Corporate and Premium Sales Department
at (800) 221-7945 ext. 5442 or by email at MacmillanSpecialMarkets@macmillan.com.

First edition, 2023

This book is set in Tonic. It was edited by Connie Hsu and Mekisha Telfer, and art directed and
designed by Mercedes Padró and Aram Kim. The production editors were Taylor Pitts and Kat Kopit, and the
production was managed by Jie Yang. The illustrations for this book were created using a mix of handmade
watercolor textures and digital art drawn in Procreate on an iPad Pro.

Printed in China by RR Donnelley Asia Printing Solutions Ltd., Dongguan City, Guangdong Province
ISBN 978-1-250-81702-0
1 3 5 7 9 10 8 6 4 2